For Audra — D. C.

To Grandma (Evelyn),

whose memory and the blanket she crocheted keep us cozy warm —R. L.

VIKING

Published by the Penguin Group

Penguin Group (USA) LLC

375 Hudson Street

New York, New York 10014

USA ✦ Canada ✦ UK ✦ Ireland ✦ Australia ✦ New Zealand ✦ India ✦ South Africa ✦ China

penguin.com

A Penguin Random House Company

First published in the United States of America by Viking, an imprint of Penguin Young Readers Group, 2014

Text copyright © 2014 by Doreen Cronin

Illustrations copyright © 2014 by Renata Liwska

LIBRARY OF CONGRESS CATALOGING-IN-PUBLICATION DATA

Cronin, Doreen.

Boom Snot Twitty / by Doreen Cronin ; illustrated by Renata Liwska.

pages cm

Summary: Three friends spend a day together, despite their very different ideas about how to spend their time.

ISBN 978-0-670-78575-9 (hardcover)

[1. Friendship—Fiction. 2. Animals—Fiction.] I. Liwska, Renata, illustrator. II. Title.

PZ7.C88135Boo 2014   [E]—dc23   2013032618

Manufactured in China

1 3 5 7 9 10 8 6 4 2

Book design by Nancy Brennan   Set in Ionic MT

Boom
Snot
Twitty

Doreen Cronin ✳ *illustrated by* Renata Liwska

Viking

An Imprint of Penguin Group (USA)

Boom, Snot, and Twitty
relaxed by the tree
and waited for the day
to begin.

"Let's go somewhere," said Boom.

"Let's stay here," said Twitty.

"Let's wait . . ." said Snot.

Boom climbed up.

Twitty stayed put.

Snot waited.

Boom got bored.

Sigh.

Twitty got tangled.

Oh my . . .

Snot did not.

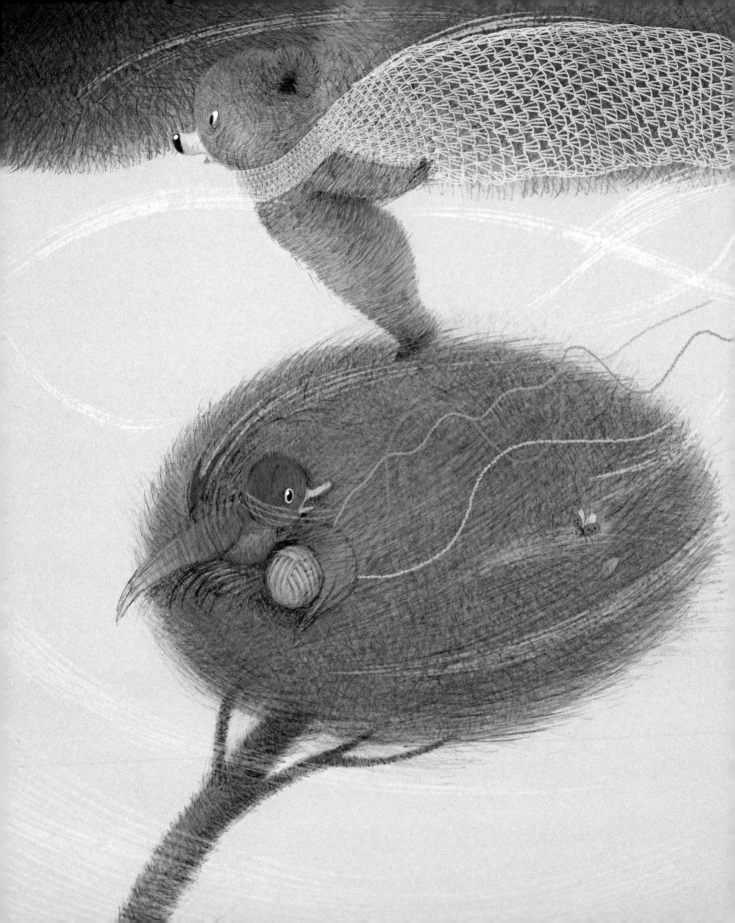

The clouds came by and the wind picked up.

"Jump!" yelled Boom.

"Hold on!" cried Twitty.

"Wind!" said Snot.

Boom jumped.

Ow!

Twitty held on.

Yow!

Snot was blown from her spot.

WHEE!

The sky got dark and the rain came down.

"Run!" yelled Boom.

"Hide!" cried Twitty.

"Rain!" said Snot.

Boom ran.

Yuck.

Twitty hid.

Yick.

Snot floated back to her spot.

WHEE!

The skies cleared up and the sun got hot.

"I'm *tired*," said Boom.

"Me, too," said Twitty.

"Sun," sighed Snot.

Boom slumped.

Twitty slipped.

Snot was happy to see them.

The sun set low and the light got dim.

"What should we do now?" asked Snot.

"Sit still," said Boom.

"Move closer," said Twitty.

Snot did not say a word.

z z z z z choo - choo